This scrapbook belongs to:

Samantha Parkington

Bon Voyage

Good-bye, New York! It's past midnight, but I'm not a bit tired. Grandmary let me stay up for the ship's launch. What a sight! The ship was lit with *hundreds* of white bulbs like a giant wonderland. There was so much confetti falling it looked like a white Christmas—in April!

Crowds and crowds of people sang "Auld Lang Syne" and toasted with champagne, just like on New Year's Eve.

A ship's steward took a picture of us with my Brownie camera.

The Admiral and Grandmary sent me this invitation to join them on vacation!

STATUE of LIBERTY

Farewell, New York!

I just about jumped out of my skin when the ship's whistle blew for departure. Everyone crowded to the rails and threw flowers into the water as the ship pulled away. The dock looked so tiny next to our giant ship.

I was sure that Aunt Cornelia, Uncle Gard, and the girls couldn't see me. But I waved to them anyway and whispered to myself, "I'll miss you!"

My cabin!

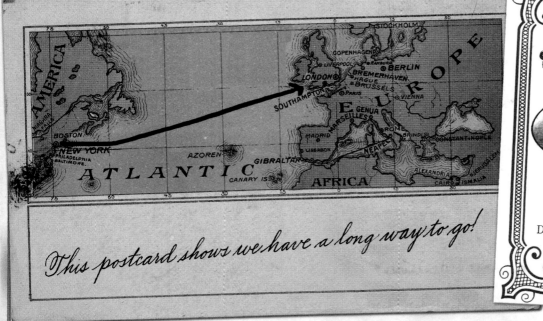

This postcard shows we have a long way to go!

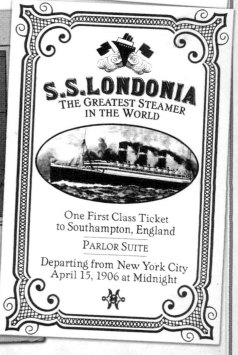

S.S. LONDONIA
THE GREATEST STEAMER IN THE WORLD

One First Class Ticket
to Southampton, England

PARLOR SUITE

Departing from New York City
April 15, 1906 at Midnight

Home Sweet Home

When we opened our cabin door, I was the first to see a gigantic basket of oranges from Uncle Gard and Aunt Cornelia. The Admiral says fruit baskets make good *Bon Voyage* presents. In the old days, sailors got a disease called "scurvy" because they didn't eat enough fruit at sea.

Grandmary thinks our cabin is small, but I think it is splendid! My bed has thick curtains that can be pulled all around it—to keep out the cold Atlantic air.

Uncle Gard can be so silly!

Orange you glad we'll be thinking of you?

Love, Gard and Cornelia

I made this rubbing of our cabin key.

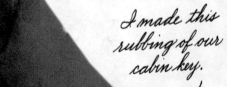

When I pull the bed curtains, I'm in a world of my own!

Our cabin has a sitting room with a writing desk and real ship's portholes! Any time we need a steward, we just ring a bell. Two rings mean "Please bring ice water." Four rings mean "Please bring hot water for our bath."

We're lucky to have our own bathroom. You have to step over a little ledge to get into it, though. Grandmary says the ledge keeps bath water from sloshing onto our carpet when the seas get rough.

Our bathroom sink and walls were made of marble!

I studied this map so I wouldn't get lost.

The Ocean Garden

Grandmary and I had tea in the Ocean Garden with the other ladies. The Ocean Garden feels just like a tropical forest. Little yellow canaries sing pretty songs in their hanging cages. Ferns and orchids are everywhere. The palm trees are so tall they nearly touch the skylight. Most of the plants are in big pots. They are bolted to the floor so they won't slide around.

Grandmary told me ladies like the Ocean Garden because they miss nature's greenery when they're at sea. She says it's the perfect place for conversation, needlework, and tea.

Too bad... My Brownie photo doesn't show all the greens and pinks and yellows.

Diana Stonebach

Ledotia Trobdrige

Julie H. Burger

The Ocean Garden

Grandmary and I had tea in the Ocean Garden with the other ladies. The Ocean Garden feels just like a tropical forest. Little yellow canaries sing pretty songs in their hanging cages. Ferns and orchids are everywhere. The palm trees are so tall they nearly touch the skylight. Most of the plants are in big pots. They are bolted to the floor so they won't slide around.

Grandmary told me ladies like the Ocean Garden because they miss nature's greenery when they're at sea. She says it's the perfect place for conversation, needlework, and tea.

Too bad... My Brownie photo doesn't show all the greens and pinks and yellows.

Aunt Cornelia would like these ladies. They are suffragists!

Our cabin has a sitting room with a writing desk and real ship's portholes! Any time we need a steward, we just ring a bell. Two rings mean "Please bring ice water." Four rings mean "Please bring hot water for our bath."

We're lucky to have our own bathroom. You have to step over a little ledge to get into it, though. Grandmary says the ledge keeps bath water from sloshing onto our carpet when the seas get rough.

Our bathroom sink and walls were made of marble!

Grandmary scolded me when I tried to move my wicker chair next to the big fountain. She said proper young ladies do *not* move furniture.

I painted a watercolor of two orchids, stitched a canary on my handkerchief, and had two cups of tea. Finally Grandmary gave me permission to excuse myself. She said I could explore the ship a bit—but only the places that are "suitable for young ladies"!

Someday I hope to paint flowers as well as my mother.

The ship's gardener takes down the birdcages and hanging ferns when the seas get rough, so they don't fall on people's heads!

On Deck

The Admiral and I blew bubbles into the sea wind!

There are so many fun things to do on the S.S. Londonia! I love playing shuffleboard and blowing bubbles with the Admiral on deck.

Every afternoon, the deck steward organizes games and races just for the children. I like tug-of-war, the three-legged race, and the egg-and-spoon race the best.

Most of the grown-ups just stroll back and forth along the promenade. Grandmary spends most of her time resting in her deck chair. The Admiral says she hasn't found her "sea legs" yet.

I'm sure glad I found mine!

S.S. LONDONIA
CHILDREN'S GAMES TODAY
FIRST CLASS DECK, 3:00 P.M.

- Tug-of-War
- Potato Sack Race
- Thread-the-Needle Race
- Biscuit-and-Whistle Race
- Three-Legged Race
- Blind Man's Bluff
- Treasure Hunt
- Egg-and-Spoon Race

I didn't even try this one!

Grown-ups relaxing in their deck chairs.

I circled the games I liked best.

These silly boys started their own game of follow the leader.

The Admiral helped me lean over the railing so I could see the red light on the *port* (left) side of the ship. Then he helped me lean over the opposite railing so I could see the green light on the *starboard* (right) side of the ship. He said all ships have these red and green lights. They help captains know whether other ships are coming toward them or moving away—especially at night or in stormy weather.

Port is red.

Starboard is green.

FIRST PLACE

I won first prize in the Egg-and-Spoon Race!

Shhh...The Library

The library is a warm and cozy place. It's so quiet you can hear the waves splashing against the sides of the ship. I love the smell of the woodwork and the leather-bound books. There are over 1,000 books here—even my favorite, *The Wizard of Oz!* I love to sit under the stained glass skylight and curl up and read.

Bon Voyage

S.S. LONDON!
DAILY NEWS UP

THURSDAY, APRIL 19, 1906. S.S. LONDONIA,

EARTHQUAKE AND FIRE: SAN FRANCISCO IN RUINS

DEATH AND DESTRUCTION HAVE BEEN THE FATE OF SAN FRANCISCO. SHAKEN BY A TEMBLOR AT 5:13 O'CLOCK YESTERDAY MORNING, THE SHOCK LASTING 48 SECONDS, AND SCOURGED BY FLAMES THAT RAGED DIAMETRICALLY IN ALL DIRECTIONS, THE CITY IS A MASS OF SMOULDERING RUINS. AT SIX O'CLOCK LAST EVENING, THE FLAMES SEEMINGLY PLAYING WITH INCREASED VIGOR, THREATENED TO DESTROY SUCH SECTIONS THAT THEIR FURY HAD SPARED DURING THE EARLIER PORTION OF THE DAY.

AFTER DARKNESS, THOUSANDS OF THE HOMELESS WERE MAKING THEIR WAY WITH THEIR BLANKETS AND SCANT PROVISIONS TO GOLDEN GATE PARK AND THE BEACH TO FIND SHELTER. THOSE IN THE HOMES ON THE HILLS PILED THEIR BELONGINGS IN THE STREETS, AND EXPRESS WAGONS AND AUTOMOBILES WERE HAULING THE THINGS AWAY TO THE SPARSELY SETTLED REGIONS. EVERYBODY IN SAN FRANCISCO IS PREPARED TO LEAVE THE CITY, FOR THE BELIEF IS FIRM THAT SAN FRANCISCO WILL BE TOTALLY DESTROYED.

DOWNTOWN, EVERYTHING IS IN RUINS. NOT A BUSINESS HOUSE STANDS. THEATRES ARE CRUMBLED INTO HEAPS. FACTORIES AND COMMISSION HOUSES LIE SMOULDERING ON THEIR FORMER SITES.

IT IS ESTIMATED THAT THE LOSS IN SAN FRANCISCO WILL REACH FROM $150,000,000 TO $200,000,000. THESE FIGURES ARE ROUGH AND NOTHING CAN BE TOLD UNTIL PARTIAL ACCOUNTING IS TAKEN.

ON EVERY SIDE THERE WAS DEATH AND SUFFERING YESTERDAY. HUNDREDS WERE INJURED, EITHER BURNED, CRUSHED OR STRUCK BY FALLING PIECES FROM THE BUILDINGS. AND ONE OF TEN DIED WHILE ON THE OPERATING TABLE. THE NUMBER OF DEAD IS NOT KNOWN, BUT IT IS ESTIMATED THAT AT LEAST 500 MET THEIR DEATH IN THE HORROR.

(continued, next page)

SUSAN B. ANTHONY GIFT

Susan B. Anthony, who passed away on March 13, has left her $10,000 estate to the women's suffrage movement.

Throughout her life, Miss Anthony campaigned actively for women's right to vote. In 1872, she was arrested and fined for voting in the presidential election.

Susan B. Anthony gave her last speech on women's voting rights in February. The speech ended with the words, "failure is impossible."

There's been an earthquake in San Francisco! We read about it in the ship's newsletter. Some of the passengers, like Grandmary's friends, the Harringtons, live in San Francisco.

Mr. Harrington has been trying to get a telegram through to his office there. Mrs. Harrington has taken to her bed with a packet of smelling salts.

I found this in the London Times!

SAN FRANCISCO BUILDING DESTROYED BY EARTHQUAKE

Poor Susan B. Anthony. Women still can't vote! Aunt Cornelia says: "If not in my lifetime, Samantha, then surely in yours." Could it really take that long?

Do Not Enter!

I *knew* I shouldn't go into the Card Room, but the door was open just a crack. Not that I could see much in the thick smoke and dim light! Some men were playing cards and dominoes. Others were smoking cigars and telling tall tales about their adventures on the high seas.

Cigars come from all over the world. The cigar bands I found are from Cuba.

S.S. LONDONIA

The Card Room is for the entertainment of our Male Guests only.

Our Female Guests may have the pleasure of visiting the Ocean Garden to take tea or partake in other ladies' leisures.

Sincerely, the S.S. Londonia

Just wait until Aunt Cornelia sees this!

Men play cards in the Card Room. Women play cards in the Ocean Garden. Why don't they just play together?

..., J'une grande curiosité.

The French man wrote this. It says:
"... little girl, with a big curiosity."

This is the money the card player gave me.

I wanted to stay in the Card Room and listen, but one of the card players caught me! He said something in French—I think it was that this room is *not* for young ladies! He said it nicely, though. He even gave me some foreign money he had won to put into my scrapbook.

Before I left, I *had* to ask the Admiral about the money. He said it was from Austria, Turkey, and France. (They use *francs* in France, not dollars.) Then the Admiral showed me the German *deutsche marks* he had won by guessing how far the ship had traveled in one day!

Ahoy Bridge!

When the Admiral escorted me out of the Card Room, he said, "If you're so curious about the ship, perhaps we should pay a visit to my friend, the Captain!"

Jimini, was I scared! I thought the Captain would throw me into the brig for being where I didn't belong! But he wasn't mad at all. He was charming, just like the Admiral! The Captain showed me how to use the compass to set the ship's course. He let me swing the big handle on the telegraph that rings a bell and sends orders to the engine room. Two bells means "full steam ahead."

The Captain uses his telescope to look for land.

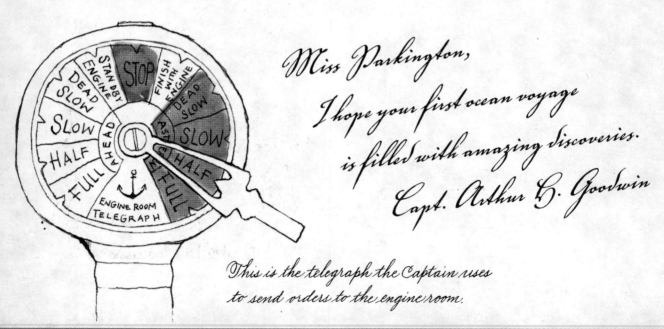

Miss Parkington,
I hope your first ocean voyage
is filled with amazing discoveries.
Capt. Arthur G. Goodwin

This is the telegraph the Captain uses
to send orders to the engine room.

The Captain also showed me the radio room. I wrote a telegram to Agnes and Agatha and I got to see the wireless operator tap out the letters in Morse code. What a fun job!

The Admiral told me Morse code was invented by Samuel Morse, the inventor of the telegraph. It uses dots and dashes to send messages from ship to shore. I'm going to practice my dots and dashes so I can learn to write messages in code!

The wireless operator listening to Morse code and writing down the words.

The wireless operator gave me a Morse code card! I'm keeping it with my first telegram.

I'm sending this message to everyone back home.

Down Below

I got bored while the Admiral and the Captain were talking about old times, so I decided to do some more exploring. I climbed down some long, narrow stairs to a big room. The room was cold and damp and noisy. The rumble of the engines was so loud I thought they must be right next door! On top of that, everyone seemed to be shouting at once—in languages I had never heard before.

I asked a girl where I was. "Oh, you're in Steerage, Miss," she said. The girl was so thin, just like Nellie the first time I ever saw her. But she smiled at me and I smiled back. She told me her name was Annie. She said she was from Ireland and that her family was going back home. They came to America just two years ago. "But nobody wants to hire my Daddy," she said. "They keep saying, 'We don't take Irish.' So we're going back."

.. -/.. .../-. ___ -
..-. .- .. .-.

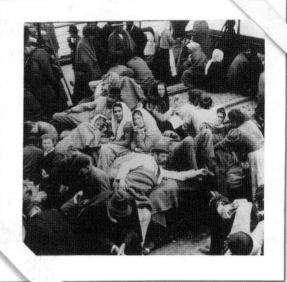

Steerage passengers have their own deck. They're so crowded.

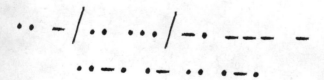

I took this picture of Annie.

Annie showed me the bunk beds where she eats and sleeps with her brothers and sisters. They eat from rusty tin plates on their laps, and are given food only once a day. If the sea gets rough, they can't open their portholes for fresh air. If they do, water splashes in.

NAME _Annie O'Callghan_

DATE **FEB 06, 1904**

HAS BEEN **VACCINATED** AND

UNLOUSED

AND IS PASSED AS VERMIN-FREE THIS DATE

SUBSEQUENT EXPOSURE TO VERMINOUS REINFESTATION RENDERS THIS CERTIFICATE INVALID, AND NECESSITATES ANOTHER UNLOUSING OF THE PERSON AND DISINFECTION AND DELOUSING OF HIS CLOTHING, PERSONAL EFFECTS, AND BAGGAGE BEFORE EMBARKATION TO THE UNITED STATES OF AMERICA.

A.A. SURGEON,
UNITED STATES PUBLIC HEALTH SERVICE

To go through this life with good manners possessed,

Is to be kind unto all—rich, poor, and oppressed.

For kindness and mercy are balms that will heal

The sorrows, the pains, and the woes that we feel.

When I told the Admiral about Annie, he gave me this card he had in his wallet.

Annie gave me this. It's the medical certificate she got when she came to America. Every Steerage passenger who goes to America has to pass a health exam.

I wanted so much to find out more about Annie. But a ship steward looked at my clothes and started shouting at me for being "out of my class." He practically pushed me back up the stairs!

Before I left, I gave Annie my blue hair ribbon. She gave me a friendship knot she had made out of twine. I am putting Annie's forget-me-knot in my scrapbook so I can remember her forever.

S.S. LONDONIA

STEERAGE MENU

MONDAY
sauerkraut, smoked bacon, potatoes

TUESDAY
pea soup, salted bacon, potatoes

WEDNESDAY
bean soup, salted meat, groats

THURSDAY
vegetable soup, beef, potatoes, rice

FRIDAY
pea soup, salted bacon, potatoes

SATURDAY
bean soup, salted meat, potatoes

SUNDAY
vegetable soup, beef, potatoes, rice

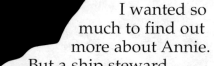

Annie's and my forget-me-knot.

Annie says her food is served from a giant tin pail. I wish she could eat with me.

..—.. · —·· ·· —· —·· / ·—·· —·—· —— —··— · · ·—· ·—·

Engines Engage!

On my way back to my cabin, a great, loud gong almost knocked me off my feet! A door right next to me whooshed open with a blast of heat. It was the boiler room—broiling hot and nearly pitch black except for the red flames of the coal fires. Two engine workers came rushing out of the room. They looked like black ghosts all covered in coal dust. And they didn't have any eyebrows—the heat had singed them off! They ran straight past me toward the cool air on the open deck. If I were those men, I'd want to get out of there, too!

The Admiral says it takes twenty-two trainloads of coal to make the steam for just one transatlantic crossing. Imagine how much black soot that makes!

This would not be a fun job!

I got all sooty!

S.S. LONDONIA

My cabin!

Annie's room is here

Grand Dining Salon

Lounge

Library

Radio Room

Crow's Nest

Kitchen and Galley

Card Room

Bridge

Crew's Quarters

Ocean Garden

Steerage Cabins

Fresh Water Tanks

Coal Chambers

Grand Ballroom

Boiler Room

Cargo

The Kitchen

Oh, if only Grandmary's cook, Mrs. Hawkins, could see this kitchen. It's huge! The pots are huge. The ladles are huge. The ovens are huge. Once lunch preparations began, I knew I had never seen so much hustle and bustle in all my life. Not even on Uncle Gard and Aunt Cornelia's wedding day!

A cook in a puffy white hat waved a large wooden spoon at me. "You mustn't stand there, Miss. They'll put you in a pot!"

On second thought, Mrs. Hawkins might not like working in this kitchen at all. She likes being the boss of her own kitchen.

The head chef telling his cooks and assistants what to do.

CONTENTS 2 QTS.

NEW YORK STATE

CUPID BRAND

GRAPES

U.S. Nº 1

TABLE GRAPES,
PACKED EXPRESSLY FOR AND SHIPPED ONLY BY
C. R. BREWER,
STARKEY, N.Y.

SENECA LAKE

CONCORD

A cook told me the S.S. Londonia has over 900 pounds of grapes on board.

A very nice kitchen worker took me aside and gave me a jam tart and a cup of tea. (I have a tea ring to prove it.) She told me it takes forty-five cooks and pantry assistants to make the meals for everyone on board. I promised her I'd sit with my tea and keep out of everyone's way!

Then she pointed to the biggest surprise—the kitchen's lobster tank. The tank provides fresh seafood for the passengers' dinners. I felt so sorry for the poor lobsters. They'd much rather be swimming in the ocean *under* the ship!

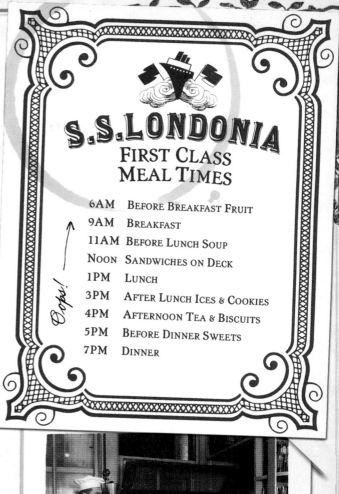

S.S. LONDONIA
FIRST CLASS MEAL TIMES

6AM	BEFORE BREAKFAST FRUIT
9AM	BREAKFAST
11AM	BEFORE LUNCH SOUP
Noon	SANDWICHES ON DECK
1PM	LUNCH
3PM	AFTER LUNCH ICES & COOKIES
4PM	AFTERNOON TEA & BISCUITS
5PM	BEFORE DINNER SWEETS
7PM	DINNER

Oops! →

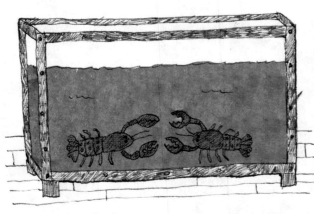

The lobsters held very still for their portrait.

The cook showed me how he goes fishing!

The Captain's Table

I got *so* excited when the Admiral told Grandmary and me that the Captain had invited us to join him for dinner. Sitting at the Captain's Table is the highest honor. When I walked into the Grand Dining Salon, I couldn't believe my eyes. It was so beautiful!

The ceiling is made entirely out of stained glass. And there is a crystal lamp in the middle of every single table. All of the chair cushions are hand-embroidered and the tablecloths are made of imported lace. I told Grandmary that the table setting is even fancier than hers—with four silver forks, two knives, a soup spoon, and five crystal glasses and goblets! (I drew a sketch so I wouldn't forget.)

No wonder people call this ship a "floating palace"!

I wish Annie could have dinner with me. I can't bear to think that her dinner is served out of a pail.

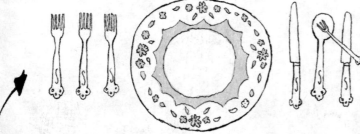

The smallest fork is for oysters. The bigger forks are for the different courses. You start with the <u>outside</u> fork.

·· · · · — · — · · — · · · — / · · · · · · — · · · — · · ———

Grandmary says the serving staff has a secret way of keeping the plates from sliding off the table. When the ocean gets rough, they dampen the tablecloths where the plates will go. Then they warm the plates before they set them down. This makes the plates stick like a suction cup.

Grandmary gave me permission to use my mashed potatoes to catch my peas when they rolled on my plate. I could *never* do that at home!

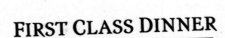

FIRST CLASS DINNER
April 19, 1906

Hors d'Oeuvres

Oysters

Cream of Barley

Salmon

Filet Mignon

Sauté of Chicken

Lamb, Mint Sauce

Roast Duckling, Apple Sauce

Sirloin of Beef

Green Peas

Creamed Carrots

Boiled Rice

Mashed Potatoes

Roast Squab & Cress

Waldorf Pudding

Peaches in Chartreuse Jelly

Chocolate & Vanilla Eclairs

French Ice Cream

This was my table place card.

Miss Samantha Parkington

It took us nearly three hours to finish eating all these courses.

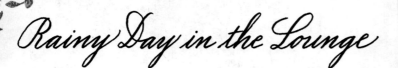

Rainy Day in the Lounge

The seas are rough today! Grandmary is feeling seasick so she went to bed. I helped her take two big spoonfuls of Mothersill's Seasick Remedy. I'm sure she'll be up in no time. I haven't felt seasick yet. The Admiral says I must have a "sailor's stomach."

We were in the lounge all day because of the weather. The Admiral played a card game called "whist" with his friends. I played Authors with the other children and won three games!

We each got to keep three Authors cards for souvenirs.

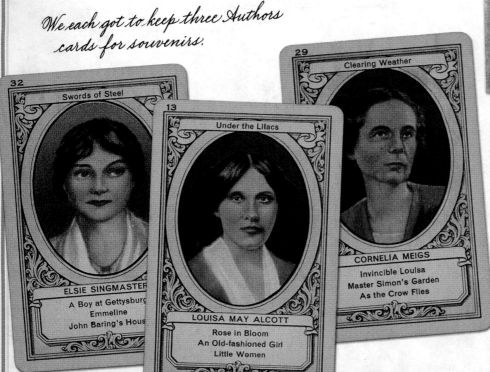

32 Swords of Steel
ELSIE SINGMASTER
A Boy at Gettysburg
Emmeline
John Baring's House

13 Under the Lilacs
LOUISA MAY ALCOTT
Rose in Bloom
An Old-fashioned Girl
Little Women

29 Clearing Weather
CORNELIA MEIGS
Invincible Louisa
Master Simon's Garden
As the Crow Flies

IN THE SW

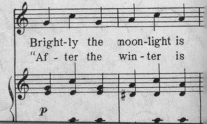

Tempo di Valse.

mf

Bright-ly the moon-light is
"Af-ter the win-ter is

p

In the evening, we had a variety show. It was so much fun! Everyone played instruments and sang. I got to sing "In the Sweet Bye and Bye." One passenger performed magic tricks with coins and scarves. Another imitated President Roosevelt talking to his pet parrot, Loretta. Best of all— Lady Chambers, a friend of Grandmary's, showed everyone how to make Japanese origami cranes.

I saved my best one.

Things I Want to Do in England...
- Climb the Tower of London
- See the Changing of the Guard
- Have tea at Buckingham Palace
- Eat some Banbury cakes
- See B... ...t Trafalgar Square

The children's steward helped us put on a puppet show.

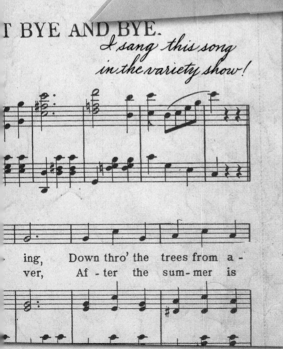

T BYE AND BYE.

I sang this song in the variety show!

ing,   Down thro' the   trees from a-
ver,   Af-ter the   sum-mer is

Dressing Day

I'm writing this while waiting for the steward to come with the hot water for my bath. It's the evening of the Captain's Gala Ball. Everyone's invited, even the children! I can't wait!

The cabin is more crowded than ever. Grandmary told me to sit on my bed and stay out of the way, but it's difficult to find space among the piles of petticoats and stockings.

The ship's laundry pressed our dresses and packed them with rose petals.

S.S. LONDONIA

The Captain and Crew

of the S. S. Londonia

cordially invite you to attend

The Captain's Gala Ball

on

April 21, 1906

at 8 o'clock in the

Grand Ballroom

What a busy place our cabin is! The hairdresser is here, weaving fresh flowers into Grandmary's hair. The steward is here, too, with my bath water. Our wardrobe door is wide open so Grandmary's and my ball dresses won't get wrinkled.

The Admiral is off having a hot lather and shave. Grandmary says it's a good thing there are barbershops on ships these days. "The last thing we need right now is a man getting in the way!"

I want to remember my beautiful dress forever!

This is a ribbon from my shoe.

The Admiral gave me a new bottle of French toilet water.

The Captain's Ball

Oh! What a glorious night! When I glided down the Grand Staircase on the Admiral's arm, I felt just like Cinderella. The musicians played softly. The decorations glimmered in the candlelight. On every table there were beautiful flower arrangements with *real* peacock feathers.

When the Captain asked to sign my dance card and escorted me to the dance floor, it was like a fairy tale. Wait until Nellie and the others hear about this!

DANCE ORDER

1 Quadrille,   Welcome

2 Contra,   Hull's Victory
Capt. Arthur H. Goodwin

3 Quadrille,

4 Contra,   Lady of the Lake

5 Quadrille,

6 Quadrille,   Belles of South Biddeford

7 Quadrille,

8 Contra,   Money Musk

Intermission 30 Minutes.

Waltz, Galop.

9 Quadrille,

10 Masquerade,   Chorus Jig
Capt. Arthur H. Goodwin

11 Waltz,

12 Quadrille,   Lancers

13 Quadrille,

14 Contra,   Boston Fancy

15 Contra,   Portland Fancy
The Admiral

After my dance with the Captain, the Admiral whispered, "Let's explore the buffet!" I told him I was too excited to eat, but he said, "Just wait!"

The buffet tables stretched across the entire room. Every dish looked like an artist's sculpture. Right in the middle was the most fantastic thing of all—a giant swan carved out of ice!

My first corsage!

The ship's stewards handed out masks for the Masquerade Dance.

Land Ho!

Our last full day at sea! The Admiral said land was near. We could hear the cries of seagulls, and the water's color had changed from dark blue to blue-green. I spent all morning on deck searching the horizon for a glimpse of land.

Finally, I heard the call from the Crow's Nest, "Land Ho!"

All of the clothes I've worn on the trip have been packed into my steamer trunk. The porters say our trunks will be waiting for us in London. I sure hope they are!

This is the label from my trunk.

S.S. LONDONIA

FIRST CLASS

NAME: _Samantha Parkington_
SAILING FROM: _New York City_
SAILING TO: _Southampton, England_
DATE: _04/15/1906_ ROOM NO.: _1_

My Favorite Things

- Staying up for the ship's launch
- Sleeping in my curtained bed
- Winning the Egg-and-Spoon Race
- Meeting Annie
- The Captain's Ball

My LEAST Favorite Things...

- Not being able to see Annie again
- Missing everyone back home
- Getting scolded for being in the Card Room and Steerage
- Sitting still for dinner
- Sitting still for tea

I have to see these things first!

WESTMINSTER ABBEY

TOWER OF LONDON
& THE TOWER BRIDGE

CHANGING OF THE GUARD

Hundreds of people crowded the Southampton dock just waiting for us. I looked all around for Annie, but I didn't see her anywhere.

The Admiral, Grandmary, and I were hustled down the gangplank so we could make the last train for London. The Admiral gave me some tiny postcards so I could decide what sights I wanted to see first.

This trip has been *so* much fun. I can't wait to begin the next part of my adventure—and I can't wait for my voyage home!

Bon Voyage!

S.S. LONDONIA
THE GREATEST STEAMER
IN THE WORLD

One First Class Ticket
to Southampton, England
— PARLOR SUITE —
Departing from New York City
April 15, 1906 at Midnight

Published by
Pleasant Company Publications
Copyright © 2002 by Pleasant Company
Produced by becker&mayer!, Bellevue, WA
www.beckermayer.com

Printed and assembled in China
02 03 04 05 C&C 10 9 8 7 6 5 4 3 2 1
The American Girls Collection®, Samantha®, Samantha Parkington®, and the American Girl logo are trademarks of Pleasant Company.

Visit Pleasant Company's Web site at: americangirl.com

Written by Dottie Raymer
Edited by Jodi Evert and Carol P. Garzona
Art directed by Will Capellaro and Jane S. Varda
Designed by Brian Fraley and J. Max Steinmetz
Cover and page 2 illustration of Samantha's family by
    Dan Andreasen
All other interior illustration by Susan McAliley
Calligraphy by Linda P. Hancock
Researched by Kathy Borkowski, Sally Wood, Dottie Raymer,
    and Carol P. Garzona
Photography by Keith Megay
Production coordinated by Mary Cudnofsky and Barbara Galvani
Special thanks to Eileen K. Morales of The Museum of the City of New York, Claudia A. Jew of The Mariners' Museum, Heather Dalgleish, Beth Lenz, Alissa Lenz, Carie Anne Taylor, and Scott Westgard.

IMAGE CREDITS

Every effort has been made to correctly attribute all the material reproduced in this book. If any errors have unknowingly occurred, we will be happy to correct them in future editions.

Key: MCNY: The Museum of the City of New York (The Byron Collection); MM: The Mariner's Museum; H/A: Hulton/Archive by Getty Images

BON VOYAGE—Statue of Liberty, Lisa Ferlick collection; Steamship, adapted from The Allan Line R.M. Triple-Screw Steamers postcard; **HOME SWEET HOME**—Detail of Interior Bedroom, S.S. Niuew Amsterdam, 1906, MCNY; Detail of Interior Bathroom, S.S. Amerika, 1905, MCNY; Map, adapted from drawings from the Titanic Historical Society Collection; **THE OCEAN GARDEN**—Palm Room, S.S. Kaiser Auguste Victoria (TMM brochure collection), MM; **ON DECK**—Passengers on Deck, S.S. Kaiser Auguste Victoria, 1906, MCNY; Detail of Children at Play on Deck, Hamburg American Line, S.S. Deutschland,1900, MCNY; **SHHH… THE LIBRARY**—Library, S.S. New York, 1988 (TMM brochure collection), MM; Earthquake, Jeff Delarm collection; **DO NOT ENTER!**—Playing card, adapted from early 1900s card, The United States Playing Card Company, Playing Card Museum; **AHOY BRIDGE!**—Man looking through Telescope, S.S. Circassia, 1896, MCNY; Wireless Operator, MM; Telegram adapted from a replica reproduced courtesy of Marconi plc; **DOWN BELOW**—On Deck, H/A; Detail of Steerage Deck, S.S. Pennland of the Red Star Line, 1893, MCNY; Third-Class Stateroom, S.S. Amerika, 1906, MCNY; **ENGINES ENGAGE!**—The Black Gang Shoveling Coal Aboard a Steamship, circa 1890, MM; Ship drawing, adapted from drawings from the Titanic Historical Society Collection; **THE KITCHEN**—Hotel Kitchens, H/A; Kitchen Fish Tank, H/A; **THE CAPTAIN'S TABLE**—Ritz Carlton Restaurant à la Carte, S.S. Amerika,1905, MCNY; **RAINY DAY IN THE LOUNGE**—Seasickness ad, *Harper's Magazine*, 1914; **DRESSING DAY**—Perfume label, unknown; **LAND HO!**—London postcards published by Valentine & Sons, Ltd.

I'll be back soon!

STATUE of LIBERTY

More to Discover!

While books are the heart of The American Girls Collection®, they are only the beginning. The stories in the Collection come to life when you act them out with the beautiful American Girls dolls and their exquisite clothes and accessories.

To request a free catalogue full of things girls love, send in this postcard, call **1-800-845-0005,** or visit our Web site at **americangirl.com**.

Please send me an American Girl® catalogue.

My name is _____

My address is _____

City _____ State _____ Zip _____

My birth date is ____/____/____ E-mail address _____
                   month day year

Parent's signature _____

And send a catalogue to my friend.

My friend's name is _____

Address _____

City _____ State _____ Zip _____

If the postcard has already been removed from this book
and you would like to receive an American Girl® catalogue,
please send your name and address to:

American Girl
P.O. Box 620497
Middleton, WI 53562-0497

You may also call our toll-free number, **1-800-845-0005,**
or visit our Web site at **americangirl.com**.

PO BOX 620497
MIDDLETON WI 53562-0497

Place
Stamp
Here

‖ ‖‖

|.|.|..||.|.|.||..||.|||..|..|.||.|.|..||.|..|..||.|

THE BOOKS ABOUT SAMANTHA

MEET SAMANTHA • An American Girl
Samantha becomes good friends with Nellie, a servant girl, and together they plan a secret midnight adventure.

SAMANTHA LEARNS A LESSON • A School Story
Samantha becomes Nellie's teacher, but Nellie has some very important lessons to teach Samantha, too.

SAMANTHA'S SURPRISE • A Christmas Story
Uncle Gard's friend Cornelia is ruining Samantha's Christmas. But Christmas morning brings surprises!

HAPPY BIRTHDAY, SAMANTHA! • A Springtime Story
When Eddie Ryland spoils Samantha's birthday party, Cornelia's twin sisters know just what to do.

SAMANTHA SAVES THE DAY • A Summer Story
Samantha enjoys a peaceful summer at Piney Point, until a terrible storm strands her on Teardrop Island!

CHANGES FOR SAMANTHA • A Winter Story
When Samantha finds out that her friend Nellie is living in an orphanage, she must think of a way to help her escape.

◆

WELCOME TO SAMANTHA'S WORLD • 1904
American history is lavishly illustrated with photographs, illustrations, and excerpts from real girls' letters and diaries.

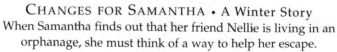